The Princess and the Pea

a traditional tale
retold by Linda Jennings

illustrated by Kay Widdowson

THERE WAS ONCE
A PRINCE WHO WANTED TO MARRY.

"Be sure to choose the right girl," said the queen. "She must be a real princess, and not someone pretending to be one."

The prince knew of no real princess in his own country, so he saddled his horse and rode off to seek her elsewhere.

The prince rode far beyond his
own land. He met many girls, fat
and thin, fair and dark. Some of
the most beautiful claimed to be
princesses, but the prince soon
discovered that they were lying.
He wondered if he could have
missed any.

Sadly, the prince returned home again.

"What shall I do?"

he asked the queen.

"Just be patient," she answered. "There is a princess out there somewhere. We'll give a ball, and send out a royal proclamation to all our neighbouring kingdoms. Only real princesses will be allowed to attend the ball."

The prince was excited. Surely, only a real princess would *dare* reply to a royal proclamation? But some girls were very good liars, as he had discovered on his travels. He could only hope for the best.

Many beautiful girls attended the ball, and the prince danced with all of them. But though they had perfect manners and danced as lightly as thistledown, the prince was unable to tell whether they were all princesses, as they said they were.

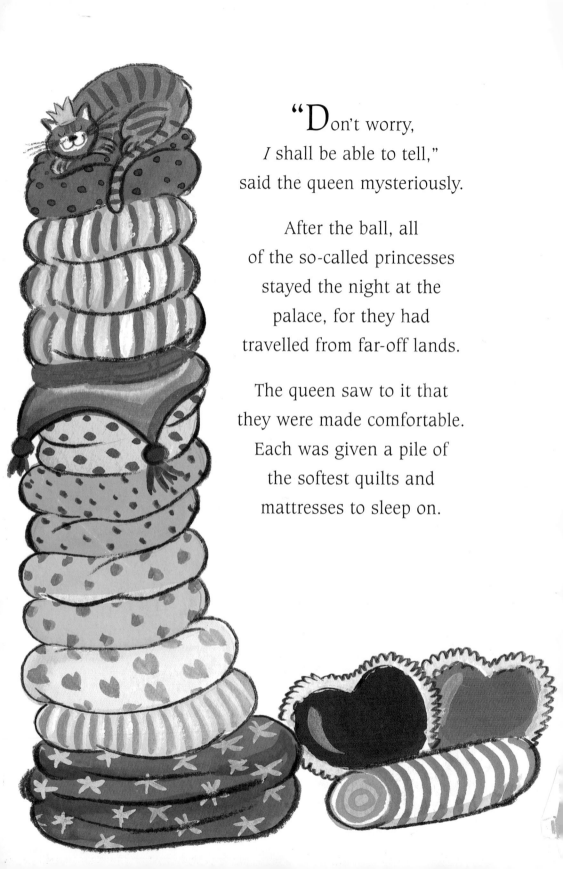

"Don't worry,
I shall be able to tell,"
said the queen mysteriously.

After the ball, all
of the so-called princesses
stayed the night at the
palace, for they had
travelled from far-off lands.

The queen saw to it that
they were made comfortable.
Each was given a pile of
the softest quilts and
mattresses to sleep on.

In the morning, the queen asked each girl if she had slept well.

"Like a dream," said one.

"I fell asleep as my head reached the pillow," said another.

"I didn't wake till the servant brought me my breakfast," said a third.

The queen frowned. "You call yourself princesses, do you?" she said. "Well you are lying, each one of you."

And with that, she sent them all packing.

"How did you know?" asked the prince, puzzled.

"You will find out soon enough," replied the queen, "when a real princess arrives."

Next day the prince went riding in the forest. Secretly he was glad about the false princesses, for he had cared for none of them. Perhaps he would find a real princess today? But though he rode for many hours, he met no one but a farmer's family on their way to market.

As the prince turned homewards, the sky darkened, and the wind began to blow.

"There's a storm coming," he said, and quickened his pace. He reached the palace just as the first drops of rain began to fall.

The storm raged all evening.
The wind blew, lightning cracked, and the
rain came down in waterfalls.

But through all the roaring thunder and
the lashing rain, the prince thought he
heard something.

"There's someone knocking at the door,"
he said.

The king shook
his head.

"Why would anyone be out on
such a night?" he asked.

KNOCK! KNOCK!
KNOCK!

came the noise, louder still.

"There *is* someone," said the prince.

He asked a servant to open the door.

Into the room stumbled a girl. She was soaking wet, and her hair lay in damp tresses around her face. Her clothes were ragged and torn.

The prince's heart gave an extra beat.

Though she was shabby, and looked as poor as a church mouse, she was the most beautiful girl he had ever seen.

"Who are you?"
asked the prince.

"I am a princess,"
said the girl. "I lost
my way in the storm."

A princess? But was she a real one?

The prince hoped above hopes that she was.

The queen ordered a room to be prepared. Just as before, the servants brought a pile of mattresses and quilts to heap up on the bed.

"I want to be sure that you will sleep well, my dear," said the queen.

The girl watched the servants pile twenty mattresses on the bedstead. On top of these, they put the twenty feather quilts.

The girl had to climb up a ladder to get into bed.

"Now we shall see!"

smiled the queen,
and she left the room.

The next morning, the royal family eagerly awaited the new guest.

The door slowly opened, and the girl appeared. Her face was white, and her eyes red. She put a delicate hand to her mouth as she tried to stop a yawn.

"You look as though you haven't slept at all well," remarked the queen.

"I thank your Majesty for your kindness to me," said the girl. "But I'm afraid I didn't sleep a wink. There was something so hard under the mattresses, that it dug right into my back."

The queen smiled and took the girl by the hand.

"My dear, I'm *so* glad you didn't sleep well!"
she said.

"Mother!" cried the prince, very shocked.
"What a way to treat a guest!"

"But now I know the truth," replied the queen.

"This is a *real* princess!

You see, I had put a pea under all those
mattresses. This is the only way to test the
truth. Only a real princess would be fine and
delicate enough to feel the pea through twenty
mattresses and twenty feather quilts."

The girl told them that she was the daughter of a king, from a faraway land. She had heard the proclamation, asking for all real princesses to attend a grand ball.

"I accepted, of course," she said. "But on my long journey here, I became lost in a storm."

"But now you have arrived, and all is well," said the prince, gazing into her eyes. For although she was pale from lack of sleep, she was the fairest girl he had ever seen, and every inch a princess!

"I shall remove the pea straightaway, and you can make up for your lost sleep," said the queen. "Later, my son, the prince, will show you the palace."

Of course, everything went well after that. The princess slept soundly on a single feather mattress, with no pea under it, and awoke refreshed.

The prince showed her the palace, and they walked together in the rose garden. He had one particular thing he wanted to say to her.

"I'm glad you're a real princess," he said. "For I wanted to marry you from the moment I saw you. Will you say yes?"

THE PRINCESS SMILED.

"I WILL," SHE SAID.

About the illustrator

KAY WIDDOWSON began her career
as an animator for children's television,
but soon moved on to illustrate
children's books.
She has worked on a range of education,
novelty and story material.
She lives in Manchester
with her partner and their five cats.

A catalogue record for this book is available from the British Library

Published by Ladybird Books Ltd
27 Wrights Lane London W8 5TZ
A Penguin Company
© LADYBIRD BOOKS LTD MCMXCIX
LADYBIRD and the device of a Ladybird are trademarks of Ladybird Books Ltd

This book belongs to